The Rifle

ALSO BY Gary Paulsen

The Rifle

by GARY PAULSEN

HARCOURT BRACE & COMPANY

San Diego   New York   London

S Paulsen

Requests for permission to make copies of any part of the work should be
mailed to: Permissions Department, Harcourt Brace & Company,
6277 Sea Harbor Drive, Orlando, Florida 32887-6777.

Library of Congress Cataloging-in-Publication Data
Paulsen, Gary.
The rifle/by Gary Paulsen.—1st ed.
p. cm.
Summary: A priceless, handcrafted rifle, carried throughout the
American Revolution, is passed down through the years until
it fires on a fateful Christmas Eve of 1994.
ISBN 0-15-292880-4
[1. Rifles—Fiction. 2. United States—History—Revolution,
1775–1783—Fiction.] I. Title.
PZ7.P2843Rh 1995
[Fic]—dc20 95-730

The text was set in Bell.

Designed by Lisa Peters

B C D E
Printed in the United States of America

481684

Dedicated to

the memory of

Scott Barrett

The Weapon

It is necessary to know this rifle.

In 1768, west of Philadelphia, a man named Cornish McManus established a new gunsmithing business. He was thirty-five years old and had been an apprentice and then an assistant to a master gunsmith named John Waynewright for nearly fourteen years. Waynewright had spent much of his life perfecting the concept of rifling—putting a set of spiral grooves down the bore of a rifle to spin and thereby stabilize the patched ball as it sped on its way—and it was said that his rifling was unique. He used a twist of one turn in forty inches, slightly faster than others who made rifled barrels, and this slight increase made the ball spin faster and become more stable, or fixed, on its trajectory.

Because rifling of a bore was, historically speaking, a relatively new concept—less than a century old—most rifles were not as accurate as they could be. But compared to smoothbore guns, which were most decidedly *not* accurate and allowed balls to wobble to the side and actually take off in a curved trajectory, rifles were an enormous improvement.

But within the field of rifling there was wide variance. Some rifles were not as accurate as others; their accuracy was based on how they were made and who made them. Many were simply utility rifles, good out to fifty or sixty yards—still much better than the smoothbores—and men were happy with that, but now and then . . .

Now and then, with great rarity, there came a blending of steel and wood and brass and a man's knowledge into one rifle, when it all came together just . . . exactly . . . right and a weapon of such beauty and accuracy was born that it might be actually worshiped.

Such rifles were called "sweet" and were, almost literally, priceless. In that time weapons were much more important than they are now—were, indeed, vital to survival, for putting food on the table, for defense, for life—and a sweet rifle was revered and adored.

What made such a rifle, a sweet rifle, so rare is that even if a gunsmith made one, achieved such a pinnacle of art, there was absolutely no guarantee that he would ever be able to do it again. It was said that a bad gunsmith could never make a sweet rifle but that even a great smith might make only one in his life.

Waynewright was a competent gunsmith and could make serviceable weapons, but he lacked the spark of genius that would make him brilliant. His rifles were plain, functional, dependable, and would never be sweet.

Cornish McManus was something else again. Waynewright often chastened him for daydreaming, for spending too much time on a rifle's form or finish, for wasting more time on silly sketches of new shapes for stocks or trigger guards—in other words, for being artistic.

The truth is that Cornish was an artist, pure and simple; he was that perfect blending of artistic thinking and force of hand that it took to make a sweet rifle.

Still, it did not come soon. Waynewright held Cornish back as long as the man worked for him. Cornish never got a chance to express himself, and the spark would have died except that in the evenings he spent time drawing on scraps of paper that he hid from Waynewright to avoid ridicule. There were new shapes for rifles, new lines, delicate filigree—all the beauty he wanted to put into his work that Waynewright held back survived in Cornish's drawings, and when it came time for him to leave and be a journeyman gunsmith, he took the drawings with him.

When he started his new shop near Philadelphia, Cornish was near penniless, and for nearly two years he worked only on bread-and-butter items—repair, retuning rifles and shotguns for hunters, making cheap trade rifles for barter with the Indians—just to get by. As it was, he barely kept his head above water and his artistic abilities were fading, perhaps would have gone altogether except for a piece of wood.

It came with a stack of rough-sawn "blanks"— dry pieces of gun-stock wood crudely hand sawn by a carpenter named Davis specifically to sell to Cornish for use in making rifle stocks. These were blocky pieces of wood only just recognizable as being for gun stocks, and usually they were of plain cherry or walnut and suitable only for rough trade guns.

Except tied in the middle of the bundle was a special piece of wood. It was six feet long, with the grain curved down naturally where the butt, or shoulder piece, came back, and when he pulled it from the bundle it seemed to come alive in his hands. The feeling was so startling that he dropped the blank back on the pile. As he picked it up again he saw that it was a slab of well-dried maple, but this was not uncommon, and it was not until he looked closer that he saw the small marks scattered over the surface of the wood and knew it was a piece of striped or "curly" maple. In the rough-sawn texture they looked almost like blemishes, scars, but he knew them at once as almost classic "bird's eyes"—tiny knots that would make the wood seem spotted and tiger striped when it was smooth-finished and oiled.

He had never seen so many of the spots and stripes, never seen such a potentially beautiful gun stock, and he decided in that instant he would make a rifle to match the stock, would make the rifle of his dreams and drawings.

And yet it did not happen fast. He still had to live, to eat, and during the days he made trade guns and did repairs and did not work on his special rifle until after the evening meal. Usually it was dark by then and he had to work in candlelight, which slowed him still more, and it was perhaps this reason, the slowness of his work, that caused him to take even more care than he would normally have taken.

Whatever the reason, he lingered over each part of the rifle with a kind of love.

Making the barrel itself took him almost six months of night work. He used his best steel strap and hot-forged it around a .30-caliber tube so that it was forty-two inches long, then bored it out to .40 caliber with a long drill bit. Using such a small bore—.40 inches in diameter—when many rifles and guns were made at .58 and even .75 inches was a change, but in his experience the smaller bore seemed to throw balls with more accuracy, and he wanted this rifle to be not just beautiful but as close to perfectly accurate as he could make it. When the blank barrel was formed and hammer-welded around the bore tube, he removed the tube and trued the barrel with a thin thread lined on all sides and down the center of the bore to make certain it was straight. Trueing alone took weeks, working late, and when he reached that stage he still did not have a finished barrel but really only one that had started.

By hand he draw-filed the outside of the barrel to have six flat sides, trueing with the thread as he worked so the flats were perfect and equal, and another two months had gone, working in the evenings in the yellow light from the candles.

Fall came and he should have gone hunting to stock up on venison for the winter, but work owned him now and each day he awakened thinking not of what he would do in the day but later, in the yellow light from the tallow candles.

With the barrel formed and the outside filed and hand-buffed, he worked at the rifling, and here again fate stepped in. He had been working with slower twists and he decided with this new rifle he would go with Waynewright's faster twist of one turn in thirty-five inches. He did not know it but it was the perfect twist for a .40-caliber bore shooting a patched ball with black powder.

The rifling was done with a long wooden rod

that had adjustable sharpened steel teeth in a fixture at one end. The rod had a spiral groove down one side that fit into a circular holder, and as the rod was pushed down into the barrel, a small metal peg engaged the groove and caused the rod to rotate as it was pushed.

Ten pushes, until the steel teeth on the rod had made the beginnings of four rifling grooves in the bore of the barrel. Then the teeth were adjusted to cut a tiny bit deeper—little more than scratches at first—and ten more pushes, then adjust, and ten more; two whole weeks of evenings until he held the barrel up to the candle and looked down to see the clean lands and grooves of finished rifling. But not quite, not quite done yet. The metal of the rifling was still slightly rough, with tiny scratches from the cutting teeth, and Cornish used a ramrod and rag soaked in lard and very fine strained sand used for blotting ink, and he polished the bore until it shone like silver—a week's work.

With the bore done, he threaded one end and screwed in a breech plug with a tang sticking back to attach to the wood and then farther up, along the bottom of the barrel, he made three cross grooves with widened bottoms to hold the metal keys that would affix the rifle to the wood of the stock.

Still the work on the barrel was not finished. Cornish buffed the steel with the fine sand and then finer sand—as fine as flour—running a rag filled with the sand-dust back and forth on the barrel until the flats seemed to be small mirrors that caught the light as he turned the rifle near the candle.

When the steel was shined and cleaned, he set it aside and went to his neighbor, who had a cow for milk, and captured two quarts of the cow's urine in a wooden bucket. Because of the smell the next step had to be done outside, and he did it the following day, taking a rare day away from his normal work time.

He heated the barrel until it was nearly red, then soaked it with a rag dipped in the urine. The steam that came up almost made him gag, but he knew what finish he wanted and he repeated the process eight times, reheating the barrel each time for a fresh coat of urine, wiping it on with the steaming, stinking, smoking rag, moving it always with the long direction of the barrel until the acids and compounds in the urine had reacted with the hot steel to oxidize it and make it a deep plum-brown color. Satisfied at last that the barrel was dark enough, he let it cool, wiped it with a clean soft rag and then another rag impregnated with refined cooking grease.

The barrel was beautiful. The grease coated and soaked into the color of the steel to make it seem deep and rich, so that he could look into the steel itself, and he wrapped the barrel in a piece of sheepskin with the wool inward and set it on a top shelf of his small shop while he worked on roughing out the stock.

He used small handsaws and chisels to carve the rough shape of the stock. It was the fashion then to have the butt, the part that went back to the shoulder, drop a great deal to give the stock a more elegant curve downward. This was the method used in Europe with guns, and many smiths in the colony copied it, thinking it made for a better weapon. In truth Cornish had found the extra drop to the stock gave the stock a sort of leverage that caused a rifle to bounce slightly up when it was fired, which diminished accuracy, and the recoil slammed backward harder because of the angle.

For this reason he reversed the principle and had the stock only drop half as much as usual. This minimized the kick of the rifle and at the same time held the barrel more steady, and while in itself it would perhaps not have made a difference, this added to the extralong barrel, small bore, and fast-twist rifling all came together to make a unique firearm.

It was still far from finished. The wood had to be grooved to let the three flats of the barrel settle in properly, and he struck a centerline and used a correctly shaped burr—a kind of push-pull chisel—to make the groove. Here he ran into trouble. The maple was seasoned to a rock hardness—some maple was actually called rock maple—and he resharpened the burr many times while cutting. Also the bird's-eyes were small knots and knots were always harder than the surrounding wood and tended to split at odd angles. Because it was so difficult he worked more slowly, and because of this, when he at last had the groove to match the barrel, he had never had such an accurate fit. The barrel seemed wedded to the wood.

Shaping the rest of the stock was more difficult yet. The rigidness of the wood and the hundreds of small knots fought him all the way, forced him to use hand rasps and files to get the curves and shapes he wanted, and when the stock was at last roughed into shape and it was time to fit the lock and trigger to the stock and barrel, he had come to nearly hate the wood for its stubbornness.

The function of a flintlock rifle was simple. Powder would be put down the bore, a patched ball on top of it pressed firmly into position, then in a little place on the lock another small amount of powder ground much finer than the powder in the main charge would be placed below a striking plate in a small cup called the pan. The hammer held a piece of flint in a small vise, and there was a tiny hole drilled from the pan through the side of the barrel into the chamber where the main charge waited. When the hammer was cocked and the striking plate (called a frizzen) was placed over the powder, the piece was ready to fire. Pulling the trigger dropped the hammer, the flint struck the frizzen, showering sparks down into the finely ground powder, which detonated and shot a piercing jet of intensely hot flame through the little hole into the main charge, which in turn set it off and propelled the ball out of the barrel.

It all sounds very slow-firing but in reality, if it is all done correctly—if the powder is dry and in good shape, if the flint is clean and with a new sharp edge, if the frizzen is wiped dry with the thumb just before firing, if the spring on the hammer is strong and slams the flint hard against the frizzen, and if the powder is positioned correctly in the pan—it is nearly instantaneous. There is no discernible pause from when the trigger is pulled and the rifle fires.

But with a flintlock there are no unimportant parts. The lock, the trigger, the position of the lock and the pan against the barrel, the strength of the springs, the speed of the hammer fall, the crispness of the let-off of the trigger—every single thing matters or the rifle will not fire correctly and, even if it somehow does, it will miss.

Since missing can mean starving or even death, no shortcuts can be taken, and Cornish went to work each night with a quiet intensity that often left him with a headache and pain in back of his eyes from squinting in the dim light from the candles.

He worked on the lock, hand filing the shape and tempering the springs, night after night until it fit perfectly in the inletted side of the stock and nestled snugly against the barrel.

The hammer he shaped with a serpentine jaw at the end to hold the flint and positioned the jaw so that it held the flint at a slight back angle from the frizzen, so that when it struck it also scraped and added to the number of sparks.

By shaping the top of the trigger in a flattened manner, he made it not to have movement. When the trigger was pulled there was an even hardness to it—he estimated three pounds—and then suddenly it let off and the hammer dropped with nothing seeming to have moved at all.

He used finely polished brass for the butt plate—ornately curved to cup the shoulder—and the patch box on the side of the butt and on the keys that held the barrel to the wood as well as the cap at the end of the wood and barrel to join them with an opening for the hole that ran beneath the barrel groove to hold the hickory ramrod. When it was all fitted and joined, he spent a month of nights smoothing the wood to a marble finish and polishing the brass until it shone like gold, and finally he rubbed warmed beeswax into the wood of the stock until the grain and the bird's-eyes seemed to jump out of the wood.

The last thing he did was to drill the tiny hole from the pan through the side of the barrel for the jet of flame to light the main charge.

And the rifle was done. It was easily the most beautiful rifle he had ever made and he thought, trying to be objective, that it might be the most beautiful rifle he had ever seen. He carefully placed it on wooden pegs covered with bits of lamb's wool over his workbench so he could see it as he worked on trade guns and repairs. Many who came to the shop saw the rifle and admired it and offered to buy it, but he was too close to it and thought it would be like selling an infant or somebody he loved, so he held back—though he could use the money because he had decided it was time to take a wife.

Besides, there remained the final test, the firing of the rifle, and strangely he was reluctant to do this, hesitated almost in a kind of fear that he would find some flaw. If it did not shoot straight, then it did not matter how beautiful it was—a rifle must work, must deliver the ball to the right place or it was worthless.

But there came a day, an afternoon when his work was caught up as much as it would ever be and the sun was high and there was no wind, a beautiful summer day, and he decided to try the rifle.

He took it from the pegs and ran a clean patch down the bore to remove any residue of grease. He selected a piece of black flint from England—the best flint still came from there—and shaped it carefully to fit the jaws of the hammer and tightened it in place, held in the jaws with a soft piece of buckskin.

He had never struck the frizzen and he did so now, cocking and letting the hammer fall on the unloaded rifle, and was gratified to see that his ideas had been right and the empty pan was virtually showered in sparks.

He had burred out a .40 mold for balls—actually making it slightly smaller so there would be room for a mattress-ticking patch—and two evenings earlier had run a hundred balls of pure soft lead. He had kept them in a small box full of rag waste so they would not roll against each other and get flat-sided, and he took the balls, the rifle, his main charge powder horn and smaller horn for priming or pan powder, and moved into the back of his shop.

His smithy was set on the edge of Philadelphia and there were no cabins farther out than his yet. There was a clearing about sixty yards across, where he kept a small garden, and he moved to the far side of it, where he had set a post for targets. On a hatchet-flattened piece of log he drew a **V**— each leg five inches high—with a stub of charcoal and tied the log vertically to his target post, and then he paced off thirty long steps.

It was close to shoot, but he knew if any errors were to show they would be easier to see at close range.

He was oddly—considering how much he loved firearms—a bad shot. He had worked at it for years, but he still wavered and couldn't get the timing right to squeeze the trigger when the sights were just right, so he didn't trust himself and always shot off a rest to make sure his own movement didn't affect the way a rifle performed.

He set up a stool with a crude table and a leather bag full of dirt to rest the barrel of the rifle on and charged the bore with a brass measure and dry powder from his horn.

He was not certain how much powder to use because it was such a small bore, but he had it in his mind that the ball should spin faster than normally, which would retard it slightly and require more powder, so he put in what would be a usual charge for a .50-inch ball.

Then he used a patch greased in bear grease, put it across the bore, and pushed the ball down— being careful to keep the "sprue," or where the mold had left a mark from pouring, straight up— to start it with his thumb, just to where it dented the patch into the barrel slightly.

He used the ramrod to push the ball smoothly down the bore to rest on the powder, setting it with a firm push—not jamming it or slamming the rod into it, which would upset the ball or give it a flat side and change the way it flew.

In all of this he took his time, though he was anxious, and it was a full five minutes before he had the rifle charged with powder in the pan and the hammer drawn back.

He had used curved-up sides, called horns, for the rear sight and a small German silver blade for the front, and he rested the barrel of the rifle on the dirt bag and settled the sights on the **V** that stood thirty yards away. He took a breath, let half of it slowly out, held it, and squeezed the trigger.

The rifle cracked—rather than the more thumping boom of the larger bores—and he was glad to note that ignition was instantaneous and the recoil straight back into his shoulder.

He could not see where the ball hit. It was too small to show the hole in the green wood this far away, but he knew that one shot didn't mean anything. It took three shots to strike a pattern, to show how a weapon would work, and he loaded the rifle exactly the same way two more times, held the sight exactly the same, and shot exactly the way he had fired before.

With the third shot he set the weapon carefully down and walked to the target and was crushed to see that there was only one hole at the point of the V where he had aimed. It did not seem conceivable that the other two balls had completely missed the log and he had a moment of almost crippling disappointment, a brief thought of all the months and months of work for something that was no more than a pretty toy. A rifle that would not shoot.

Then he saw that the side of the bullet hole seemed odd, smudged and pulled slightly to the side, not the neat round hole that a ball should make.

Could it be possible, he thought—could more than one ball have gone in the same hole? With trembling fingers—he had never heard of such a thing, a rifle so consistent and accurate that it shot in the same hole—he used a small chisel to clear away wood and bits of splintered lead, and when he was done he found not two but three balls smashed, swaged into the log one almost exactly on top of the next.

He couldn't believe it, thought it must be some kind of fluke. Perhaps he had used a bit of log with balls already fired into it—though he knew he hadn't, he still could not believe what had happened. He decided to try it again with a fresh piece of wood and he did so, taking care to aim deliberately and squeeze the trigger slowly, and this time there was no doubt.

The hole was not quite true, almost two balls wide, but all three of the balls had gone in virtually the same place and he knew that he had done something very grand in making this rifle, and that evening while he cleaned it with warm water and regreased the bore with strained bear grease to keep rust from happening, that night he knew he would never be able to sell it.

But the rifle was not the only thing to enter

Cornish's life then. The day after he found how sweet the rifle was—shooting three balls in the same spot—the next day he met Clara.

It was not love at first sight. Clara was too practical for that. She came with her father to pick up his fowling piece that Cornish had repaired. Cornish could not take his eyes off Clara and when he smiled at her and nodded, she smiled back in a way that meant so much.

Cornish came to call, and then came to court and sit on a bench and watch the evening sun set with Clara, and when he asked for her hand she said yes and her father said yes and Cornish knew he would need money to start a family.

He had nothing to sell except the rifle.

At the back of his workbench on the wall he had pegged the two target logs with the holes showing and had the rifle lying across them and he had stopped counting the men who came and wanted to buy it. Always he felt a pang—as if they wanted to buy his son or daughter—and always he said no, no, he would keep it a while.

But now it was different. Now there was Clara and their new life, and he decided to sell the rifle. Still he felt it should not just be a work gun, not a gun to have nearby when you plow. This rifle, he thought, was destined for something more, some great thing, and he was thinking this one morning, only three days before they posted the wedding banns, when John Byam came into his shop. Outside, Cornish could see two horses, one with a saddle and one with packs bundled and covered with heavy, greased canvas.

Byam had a rifle but it was an old Pennsylvania—large bore—and the rifling was nearly gone from constant rubbing with the ramrod. More than many men, John lived because of his rifle. He was a young man, unsettled and given to running the ridges and country of the west—into western Pennsylvania and even beyond. He did not speak much, wore buckskins that smelled of wood smoke and deer blood, and walked in moccasins so worn his feet could nearly be seen through them. He didn't speak much but when he handed his rifle over to Cornish to get the rifling rebored to a larger size, he looked up and saw the sweet rifle on the two target logs.

"Made with your hands?" he asked.

Cornish nodded.

"Is it a good piece?"

"It's a sweet shooter, very sweet."

"Is it offered?"

Cornish nodded slowly, against his will. "It depends. What can you offer?"

He whispered, almost a hiss. "Anything I have."

Cornish had been looking down at Byam's rifle and the intensity in his voice made Cornish look up suddenly. "You know rifles?"

Byam ignored him. "Might I see . . . hold it?"

For a moment Cornish hesitated, then took the rifle down and handed it to Byam. Byam looked at the barrel. "It's small . . ."

"Because it's meant to be small. The size of the ball is balanced . . ."

" . . . by the speed and accuracy." Byam nodded.

"I have thought a smaller bore is better, but nobody makes them. Or did. Does it shoot as pure as it looks?"

Cornish pointed to the two target logs. "Three balls in each hole."

"How far?"

"Thirty paces."

"Can I shoot it?"

Again Cornish hesitated, but he thought of Clara and the need to sell the rifle—and then too there was something about this young man, this Byam. He didn't just hold the rifle so much as fit with it in some way, as if the weapon were simply an extension of his arms, his body.

Cornish nodded. Byam expertly ran a dry patch down the bore of the rifle, poured powder from his own horn into the cupped palm of his hand for a measure, poured it down the barrel, took a patch from his bullet pouch and a ball from Cornish, seated the ball, turned the rifle away, stepped outside, and aimed into the woods and opened the frizzen, tapped a few grains of fine powder into the pan, and raised the rifle, aimed across the clearing. "The white limb, that dead one. I'll cut it."

Cornish squinted, then saw it—it had to be eighty paces. Even from a rest he couldn't hit it and he doubted this Byam could. "Shoot closer—"

Before he could finish, the rifle cracked and Cornish saw the limb jerk and fall to the ground.

"Sweet," Byam said, nodding. "Like honey from a tree after a long, dead winter. "I'll buy it."

"We haven't discussed worth," Cornish said. "Now the way I view it . . ."

"On my packhorse I have all my cured hides from last season. A year's work. The pack is yours for the rifle. And I'll give you my old one."

Cornish thought a moment. That was easily twice what the rifle would bring from anybody else, and Byam took the hesitation wrong, took it as a negative answer and added, "I'll throw in the packhorse as well. The rifle must be mine."

Cornish sighed. "It isn't the price, it's the rifle. I'm fond of it."

"You can make another."

"Not like this one. No, I cannot."

And Byam grew quiet because they both knew it was true. If he lived to be a hundred, Cornish would never again come close to the sweetness of this rifle. Still, he was to marry Clara and he needed a start. "Done. You keep the horse."

"No, I said it and I meant it."

"That would not be fair. You keep the horse and I'll take the pack, as you said first. That will be enough and more than enough."

And the business was done. Byam unloaded the packhorse and took the rifle and ball mold, a small keg of powder, and twenty pieces of black flint, and left; and not once during the transaction did Cornish take his eyes off the rifle and even when Byam left, rode off into the woods leading the packhorse with the rifle across his lap, even then Cornish watched it, watched the rifle until the trees closed in and he could not see it any longer. Nor was it done yet. He missed the rifle and over the next days found himself looking up where it had hung,

expecting to see it and disappointed, almost griev-
ing when he didn't. At last he said to himself, half
aloud, "Enough. He's gone in the woods and probably dropped the rifle off a cliff by now."

He was wrong. Nothing happens in a vacuum.
While he worked on the rifle Cornish was in fact
destined to meet Clara and fall in love, and while
he worked on the rifle, England—riddled in fear
that the colonies in America would grow to dom-
inate and outproduce and take over the world,
which in fact is exactly what happened—began to
add taxes to Colonial produce and products to try
to hold them down. With this they forbade the
Americans to sell anywhere but to certain markets
in England where the prices were kept viciously
low, and compounding the problem they threw an
added tax on tea that was little more than coupling
insult to injury.

While Cornish worked on the rifle some men
in the American colonies rioted, some died, shot
down by British soldiers; some men met in a hot,
muggy meeting hall in Philadelphia and discussed

a declaration one of them, a man named Jefferson, had penned proclaiming independence from England or any form of tyranny.

All of this led to a war. The Americans called it a War of Independence, a Revolutionary War, but to England it was simply a revolt.

Had John Byam continued moving back into the woods, none of this would have affected him, nor the rifle. But as he left Cornish, knowing almost nothing of what had been transpiring for the past two years, having lived in the wilderness as he had, he came to a fork in the trail that led to the right, and even this may not have mattered except that it was on this same day that the British soldiers found stored powder and lead on the Bainbridge farm.

Byam's trail led to the Bainbridge farm and he knew the Bainbridges slightly as a quiet couple who spoke little and worked hard. He had stopped there and been given a hot meal on the way in— as, indeed, the Bainbridges provided for all travelers who passed by. Bainbridge was a nice man, and in fact it was this niceness that led him to trouble. Men had come in the night, men with tired horses and a wagon with shrunken and loosened spokes, and asked to bury their cargo—several hundredweight of lead and coarse-ground cannon powder—at the Bainbridge farm until they could come back for it. Bainbridge could have guessed the powder was for cannon, could have known it was to be used to fight the British, but he ignored it and simply nodded. He was, after all, American before he was British—why shouldn't he help?

But somebody talked and a contingent of British soldiers came just an hour before Byam and found the store of munitions.

Their laws were strict and plain: anybody caught helping the rebels with food, horses, shelter, and especially arms was subject to summary justice without trial and immediate execution by hanging.

As Byam started into the clearing, roughly two hundred yards from the house, he saw two soldiers setting Bainbridge on top of a horse with a rope around his neck and his arms tied to the rear. His wife was standing to the side, her hands clasped in front of her mouth in a double fist, two soldiers in red coats holding her.

Byam did not think about what he was doing except to know that somehow he could not let Bainbridge be hanged. The rifle snapped up, almost by itself; the tiny blade of the front sight settled on the officer sitting on his horse nearby, the sight raised slightly to compensate for distance, and the rifle cracked—one clean, smacking slap of sound across the clearing.

The ball took the officer in the throat, just below the Adam's apple, cutting through at a transverse angle to snap the spine and whip the man from his horse as if hit by a giant hand. He was dead before he hit the ground.

The action did not save Bainbridge. The sound of the rifle startled the horse he was sitting on and it jumped forward, out from beneath Bainbridge, who pitched at an angle and broke his neck and hung there dying while for a stunned second a half-dozen British soldiers looked from Bainbridge kicking and dying to their officer, who was already dead and broken on the ground, and then up to the cloud of smoke that hung where the rifle had fired.

But the surprise was only for an instant. They were, after all, soldiers and used to reacting to danger, and quickly the sergeant assumed command and pointed at the smoke. Byam was hopelessly out of range for the smoothbore weapons of the soldiers to have any accuracy, but they raised and fired on command and he heard the balls whistling as they went past him, over him, two skipping in the dirt well out in front of him, and he also heard a grunt as one of the balls hit his horse high in the chest.

The wound was mortal. Byam could feel the horse sagging and he jumped free of the saddle as the animal hit the ground and then things began to happen very fast. The soldiers all had horses and they mounted, headed out across the field toward Byam.

He could reload, he knew, and perhaps get two of them before they closed on him but that would leave four and they would get him. He pulled a long-bladed knife from his belt and slashed the empty packsaddle from the packhorse, grabbed the mane with one hand, and swung up bareback. There was no time to change the saddle from the dying horse to the packhorse. No time now for anything but running. He threw one quick look at the farmstead where Bainbridge's wife—now a widow—was trying to untie the rope holding her husband, then to the six mounted soldiers galloping at him across the field, and he wheeled the packhorse, steering with his knees, and tore off directly into the woods, off the trails.

As it was they nearly took him. Byam hadn't time to reload, nor do anything but run, holding the rifle with one hand and the horse's mane with the other, slamming the horse's ribs with his heels, wishing he had spurs.

The English soldiers did have spurs and raked their horses to more speed and would have caught Byam except that he suddenly felt the horse drop out from beneath him into a ten-foot-deep ravine.

The packhorse was surefooted after all the mountain work he had done trapping and he landed cleanly, pivoted, and ran off down the floor of the ravine as if he'd been doing it all his life.

The English horses were not so good and the ravine proved a disaster for three of them, breaking their legs on impact. One other horse was badly sprained and most of the riders were knocked senseless. Two of them were all right, the sergeant and one private, but the sergeant shook his head and killed the chase. It was just as well, for the private remembered the shot Byam had taken across the field and had absolutely no desire to tear off after him with only one man.

Byam went free.

And once more fate took over. Had he simply melted back into the woods he would have been fine. The soldiers were never close enough to identify him, were from another sector and on temporary duty. Byam would have vanished into obscurity.

But when he'd ridden hard for an hour—he

thought six or eight miles—he burst into a smaller clearing, perhaps eighty yards across, and found himself the center of attention for nearly a hundred well-armed men all dressed in green with fringed coats, who all seemed to be aiming rifles at Byam.

He wheeled the horse to a stop and slid off. Whoever they were, they weren't British, and when one of them stepped forward Byam faced him openly.

"Do you have a name?" the green-coated man asked.

"Do you?" Byam said by way of an answer. He reloaded while he spoke, seating the ball. He was not yet certain the British soldiers weren't coming and he wanted to be ready if they should suddenly burst upon the scene.

"I am John," the man said and Byam grinned.

"I am as well."

"Are you a loyalist?"

Byam shrugged. "I don't know. I've been in the forest and don't know the names."

"Do you favor the British or the fight for independence?"

"I know nothing of this independence you speak of, but I do not favor the British." Byam looked back the direction he'd come. "There are some after me."

This caused a stir in the men. They quickly led their horses out of the clearing into the brush at the sides except for the leader, who stayed with Byam and asked many questions about the British—how many, how they were armed, how mounted, why they were after Byam. And here Byam decided it was all right to tell the truth.

"I shot an officer, that's why they chase me." He quickly told the story of Bainbridge being hanged and how he had fired.

"How far?" the leader asked. "I know—knew Bainbridge well. He was a good friend who fed me often and I know his place. Where were you and where was the officer when you fired?"

Byam told him.

"That's two hundred paces if it's a foot," the leader said. "Are you certain?"

"I have had the rifle but one day and do not know it well yet, but I can tell you that I have never seen or heard of a sweeter one."

"May I see it?"

Byam held for a beat and then nodded. He was completely surrounded by men with rifles and guns. If they chose to take him it would be over in a second. He handed the rifle over.

The man nodded, held the rifle for a moment, and then handed it back without looking at it. He hadn't cared about the rifle so much as the fact that Byam would hand it to him—a kind of test.

"Who are you?" Byam asked, taking the rifle back into his hands. "And why do you fight the British?"

"We are volunteers—McNary's Rangers. I am McNary. And we fight the British for independence—for a free America."

Byam was surprised. "How did this come

about? America without England? How can that be?"

"How long were you in the western forests?"

Byam frowned, thinking. "Two years and a bit more. I came out once to go to a trader, but there was no talk of fighting the British."

"Well there is now. And like it or not you're in the thick of it—killing a British officer. They'll be hunting you hard."

Byam looked back the way he had come. "I'm not an easy man to catch."

"Still, they'll come for you. Why not ride with us?"

"You?"

"What's against it? We eat when we can, fight when we can—and there's safety in numbers. We're a hard-moving, hard-fighting set of volunteers."

"Where are you bound for?"

"South. General Washington is down by New York and we thought to join him there and help the cause. We could use another rifle, especially if you can shoot the way you say you can."

"Is there a saddle for me? I had to leave mine when they shot my horse."

"A saddle, cup, spoon, and bowl—and all the dry powder and pure lead you'll need."

"Well then, done and done," Byam said. "It sounds right."

And so it proved to be, at least for a time. Byam took the saddle they gave him—and the spoon, cup, and bowl—and joined them on the ride to New York.

Had they ridden straight through and the roads been good they might have done it in ten days to two weeks.

But it rained and the roads were little more than mud trails and they constantly ran into British patrols. Usually the patrols were small and they brushed them aside after brief fighting—little more than hit-and-run skirmishes—and always the rifle of Byam spoke and always one or two British officers went down, taken cleanly and often at long ranges.

Once they encountered a full company of British regulars who gave them a stiff fight and would have done more damage—the rangers lost three men killed and six more wounded—but the British were on foot and the rangers escaped on their horses before they could be pinned down.

As it was, the trip to New York took close to six weeks—rain, mud, and fighting all the way— and when they arrived they found Washington locked in a stalemate that was little more than trench fighting.

Sitting in mud trenches to fight a long-suffering war where an enemy you couldn't see lobbed mortar and cannon shot into you at odd intervals did not suit the free-roving spirit of the volunteers and they chafed at the bit to be loosed to fight their own way.

All, that is, but Byam. The situation was almost perfect for his abilities. The British and Colonial lines were three hundred yards apart, give or take a bit of wobble in trenches, and the static fighting meant that men grew careless. The English simply couldn't believe it possible to shoot a rifle—or what they called a gun—more than eighty or ninety yards and they viewed the distance between the trenches as being three times as far as a gun could shoot. Consequently, they often stood and exposed themselves to possible fire, believing they were safe.

The officers seemed to be particularly arrogant and would sit their horses well above the trenches, seemingly believing they were bulletproof, and Byam, as one of the Colonial militiamen put it, "mowed them down like summer grass before the scythe."

That they did not learn amazed him. Almost daily he took an officer or sergeant, Byam moving along his own trenches, waiting quietly, sipping fresh water, and chewing on a piece of bread until at last the perfect shot came to him, three hundred—once just under four hundred—yards away, an officer sitting on a horse, looking through a brass telescope or scanning a map.

The rifle would come up, settle on the log bulwark at the front of the trench, and poise while Byam aimed and squeezed. Then the crack—high-pitched, keening—and the jet of smoke and a second later the officer slumped or fell or was pushed back by the ball hitting a bone on its way through.

Once three officers. The first one down, then he would reload while they stayed to help the dead one, and a second one down, and finally the third one, taken as he swung to look at the American lines, knowing that it wasn't an accidental shot, that he was the next, and then he was down as well.

Byam was, completely, deadly—so much so that a prisoner taken in by a patrol said that the British high command was told to instruct officers heading for the front to make certain their wills were done and all things were in order with their families for surely they would die because the "ruffian Americans" did not know how to fight properly and were crudely aiming their fire at the officers "with telling effect."

And there was truth in the statement. Militiamen fighting in the Continental army recognized that the British fought rigidly, following the commands of their officers so closely that one man jokingly said if the front rank walked off a cliff the whole regiment would follow them. It was perhaps not that bad, but they were very attuned to what their officers told them to do, and the Americans quickly found that if the officers were gone the men acted in some confusion.

Not all the Americans had rifles—although a good many did—and of the ones who had rifles not one in a thousand shot as sweet as Byam's. But they were all, almost to a man, accustomed to living with a gun and their weapons were staggeringly more accurate than those of the British. In fact many of the British soldiers thought there was something unnatural about it, some strange and savage thing that allowed Americans to hit so well.

And hit they did. Byam was probably the best, but there were many—hundreds—who were also sharpshooters, and they aimed first at officers—always at officers.

"It is death for an officer to raise his head," one lieutenant wrote home. "Balls come thick as bees."

Soon Byam's ability—and his rifle—were legendary. He was fast becoming a folk hero and everybody wanted to know the gunsmith who made the rifle. Byam told them but by this time the British had found Cornish, decided he was a traitor to the Crown and making rifles for the Revolution, and made Clara a widow by hanging him to the tree outside his gun shop.

Nor would Byam fare much better. Most soldiers died not of wounds from battle but from dysentery and the resulting dehydration from diarrhea. (This was true later in the Civil War as well and was only stopped when the women—mothers of soldiers—objected and made the army "discover" hygiene and sanitary food preparation.)

Byam drank dirty water and contracted dysentery. Two men helped him to the rear where a dugout had been fashioned for the sick. He lay fevered and dirty for three days—the rifle near him, held by him for almost the entire time—and then died while suffering agonizing cramps.

Byam was buried in a grave with seven other young men who had died of illness, covered with quicklime to dissolve the body—the thinking was it kept the disease from spreading—and his history ends there.

But the rifle continued. One of the men who helped him to the dugout came back when he heard Byam was dead and asked after the rifle. A middle-aged lady named Sarah told him it was gone but she lied.

She knew something of rifles. Her husband—before his death some years earlier—had run the woods like Byam, and she had heard of Byam's rifle and what he had done.

She had two sons who had just joined the Continental army and had taken the rifle for one of them. But they never saw the rifle because they were both killed by an exploding artillery shell the day before she was to meet them.

In grief she went home to her now empty farm in what would become Connecticut. She took the rifle with her and without much thought put it between timbers in her attic and promptly forgot it.

She did not do well. The death of her sons left her in a permanent air of despondency and within the year she died—it was said of a broken heart—and without any heirs (neither of her sons had married and she had no daughters); the house was sold at public auction.

A wealthy bachelor bought it, moved in, and lived his life without ever looking in the attic. He died in 1843, and left no heirs as well. Again the house was sold at auction, this time going to an elderly couple who also did not look between the rafters in the attic, and after them another middle-aged couple, then it became a play cottage for a wealthy New York family, who held it for three generations—never checking the attic—until it was sold to an editor from a New York publishing firm.

It was now 1993, and the editor had two children—a boy and a girl, the girl eight and the boy ten—and it was they who eventually sneaked into the attic and discovered the rifle.

It had surprisingly little damage for so long a time. Byam had kept it greased, rubbing the grease well into the wood and steel. So many times had he done this that the metal and wood both absorbed the grease and made it impervious to outside damage. The grease had dried but still protected, and when the editor wiped the rifle with a damp rag the steel and bird's-eye pattern in the wood shone in the light.

He wanted to hang the rifle over the charming stone fireplace—"it looks so . . . so American," he said—but his wife hated guns, even old guns, even old guns that she agreed might be antique and seemed to be pretty, and at last he agreed.

"Get rid of it," she said. "Right away. I don't want a gun in this house."

He found it hard to make the gun go away. He thought of selling it but didn't know who would buy it and suspected it might be illegal anyway. Finally he went to an antique store and sold it there for twenty-five dollars—"It's just a piece of junk," the store owner said, "not worth more . . ."

But he lied. He sold the rifle two days later for two hundred dollars to a man from Kansas City who was on a trip and who was a collector of firearms. The Kansas City man knew something of guns and suspected this might be a good rifle but didn't know for sure as there was no date on the weapon.

It didn't matter because he fully intended to sell the rifle at a gun show in Arkansas on his way home for three or four hundred dollars and take his profit and that was, precisely, what he did. He allowed himself to be haggled down to $350 and counted it a good sale, selling the rifle to a man approximately thirty-five years old, who had hair cut very short and was wearing a baseball cap with a National Rifle Association emblem on it and a vest with slogans sewn on the back dealing with several aspects of gun ownership:

I'll give up my guns when you pry them from my cold, dead fingers.

And:

If guns are outlawed only outlaws will have guns.

And:

Register criminals, not guns.

His name was Tim Harrow. He was thin with a slight gut from drinking beer, and he ate, smelled, and lived for guns—buying and selling them, owning them, shooting them, repairing them, and endlessly, endlessly discussing them with other gun owners and enthusiasts who knew as much and also talked. Tim possessed an extraordinary amount of knowledge about guns and ballistics—bullet weights, muzzle velocities, energy on target, punch, effective range versus accurate range, what the curve of a bullet's nose was called (the *secant ogive*), how much a bullet of which rifle dropped in a hundred yards, chamber pressures, how much a bullet expanded on impact with flesh, with bone, what size weapon it took to stop what size game (including man, which he thought of technically as another form of game: "A nine-millimeter is kind of light for a big man—it'll kill him but not put him down like a magnum").

Staggering amounts of information concerning weapons and their use swirled through his head, and with it there were certain aspects of the Constitution and history and a large measure of Christ and Christianity as he thought of it so that it all rolled into one philosophy in some way he could not define but knew, was absolutely certain, was the only right way to view things.

It was, for instance, entirely possible and in his own mind completely logical for Tim to equate killing an intruder—he would call it "using justifiable deadly force"—with freedom of speech, Christ's teachings, and an understanding of the technical aspects of the weapon being used to kill the intruder, including where the bullet would hit and what the effect (the "hydraulic shock") of impact would be, mixed in with a dose of sentences from the Constitution pertaining to rights to privacy and the right to keep and bear arms.

Nor was any of this in the least confusing to Tim or any of the thousands of men—and some women—he talked to at gun shows and swap meets.

Tim viewed himself as a conservative who believed in the Flag and the Country, hated taxes—to the extent that he wanted to stop income taxes and had actually once said, "Jesus would not want us to pay taxes"—and wanted to stop welfare completely "except, of course, for the old people." With this conservative view he also held the belief that he would use his guns—the number and type fluctuated constantly but he never had less than twenty-five or thirty rifles, shotguns, handguns, and surplus military weapons—to defend the country and die doing so if need be. He viewed the government in some obscure way as an enemy of the people—especially Big Government, as he thought of it, somehow ignoring that it was made of people—and spent a lot of time trying to avoid being controlled or watched or even known by the government.

For that reason he lived entirely on the move, in a large motor home, never claimed any of his income, never paid taxes, and operated as a kind of underground gypsy, selling and buying guns and sometimes knives—which he called "edged weapons."

As far as the government was concerned, once he separated from the army—with an honorable discharge after serving three years at Fort Bliss, Texas, as a clerk—he ceased to exist.

Had he known the history of the rifle—how it had been part of the Revolutionary War, how Byam had used it—he could easily have worshiped it. In his life, in all his life—or virtually all the lives of all the thousands and even millions of men who were weapons enthusiasts, who believed in the right to keep and bear arms, who swore that they would be unsafe without a weapon, in all his life he would never need a gun nor use a gun to defend himself or his property. Even police officers, constantly working in the area of crime and danger, almost never fired their weapons against men. Tim was at far more risk—it would indeed kill him when he was forty-six in a horribly slow and painful death—from stomach cancer from the carcinogens in the beer he drank each evening after he parked to camp; the cancer viruses were much more an actual enemy than any suspected intruder and it was ironic that Tim spent so much energy on defending himself with weapons and ignored the larger danger of drinking, which would kill him.

To actually own a weapon, to hold a rifle in his hands that had been used to help make the country would have been almost too much for Tim to stand—akin to meeting George Washington.

But Tim knew little of actual history except for an extremely focused idea of how guns figured in it. He knew what weapons Custer and his troopers carried, for instance, but not how they fit historically—that the troopers' rifles frequently jammed after one or two shots and the handguns were hopelessly inaccurate past twenty or so yards, or that a large number of the Indians were better armed than the troopers and that many of the troopers tried to surrender and handed their weapons to the Indians, or that all the troopers went into battle wearing straw boater hats (barbershop quartet hats) because their issue hats were inadequately manufactured by crooked companies and they had to buy their own and the straw boaters only cost a dime and kept the sun out of their eyes, or that all of them were very small men, selected that way so as to not tire horses—none of this was known to Tim. He knew only that the troopers carried .45–.70 carbines and single-action Colt revolvers and—in his thinking—they had all died bravely "with their boots on" defending Tim's specific idea of the American ideal.

Had he known the true identity of the rifle but then been told that the original owner—a true Revolutionary War hero—died of dysentery on dirty straw spread on an earth floor, Tim would simply have remembered the first part and put the knowledge of the second part in the back of his mind and forgotten it.

But he didn't know what the rifle was or where it came from, knew nothing of John Byam or how sweet the rifle shot or how many British officers it sent down.

He just knew it was old and might have some value, and he thought he would keep it, at least for a while. So he sprayed it lightly with preservative oil, including a squirt down the bore, wrapped it in a moisture-absorbent cloth, taped it all together, and propped it in the back closet of his motor home, and by the time he'd gone a hundred miles down the road heading west his thoughts were off the rifle and on to the day's news, where he heard that a large religious encampment in Texas had been raided and burned and all the people killed in the action. He knew nothing except that they had been religious fundamentalists and had stored large numbers of weapons, and he could not see how that was grounds for an attack by the government—he viewed himself almost exactly the same as the Waco people—and made a mental note that it was just another reason to hate the government and what they were doing to people.

He had forgotten the rifle completely by the time the news special was over and again the rifle seemed to be destined to spend a long time in dark storage.

But everything counts in the timeline of history. Every little thing becomes absolutely vital to the future. So it was that if John Byam had not swallowed dirty water he might have lived many more years, or he might have died in combat, or of tuberculosis—which killed hundreds—or even died on a later day and that would have changed the time flow of the rifle and made its history totally different.

Just as now another slight bend in fate occurred. As he moved through a small town in Missouri the fuel pump on his motor home decided to give up the ghost and the huge machine stopped dead at an intersection next to a gas station.

It could have happened anywhere, anytime, but it didn't. It happened almost in the driveway of the gas station and the man who owned the station was also an excellent mechanic. His name was Harvey Kline but everybody who liked him called him Harv, and since everybody who knew him seemed to like him, that had become his name.

He used a tow truck to pull the motor home up into the station parking area and soon found the problem was the fuel pump.

"How much to fix it?" Tim asked, and was stunned when, after calling the parts stores, Harvey said, "With labor it will come to close on four hundred dollars."

"That's too high."

"The pump is over three. I'm not making much on labor."

"I can't afford it."

This was a blatant lie. Tim had over twenty thousand dollars in cash and gold in the motor home, hidden in small bundles. But he lived in cash and he hated to spend it and he just knew that he could somehow dicker the price down or do a little bartering. "Would you take a trade?"

"What have you got to trade?" Harv asked, openly skeptical.

For a second Tim hesitated, but they were standing inside the station and he saw a picture on the wall showing a fresh-scrubbed Harv with his wife and two children, a boy eleven or so and the girl perhaps six or seven.

"Nice family," Tim said. "That's what makes America great—families." And then the rifle popped into his head. He fought for the connection. Families, American, rifle—and he had it. "Family like that, you ought to have something for the future, something that will grow in value."

"What have you got?"

"Just a minute, I'll get it." He went to the motor home and found the rifle in the back closet, took the rag off, and wiped it until it shone and carried it back into the garage.

"This is a true antique, a collector's item. It's

worth over seven hundred dollars now and will continue to grow—there just aren't any more being made."

"It's just an old gun," Harv said, shrugging. "Heck, they're all over the place."

"This one"—Tim took a breath and lied, or thought he was lying—"was carried by a soldier in the Revolutionary War."

"No—you're kidding."

"It's a fact. I've had it for years, passed down in my family." All lies, only based on a truth Tim didn't know, as he didn't know that the true worth of the rifle, if it were documented and being in the good shape it was in, might be in the neighborhood of ten or fifteen thousand dollars.

But if Tim was ignorant of the value of the rifle, Harv wasn't. In a backward kind of way he understood the worth of the rifle, or at least hoped the rifle had worth that would grow. In truth, he was looking for something, anything that he could put money or work into that would grow and maybe help to save funds for his children when they went to school. That's how he thought it: I need funds for the children's college.

But he was a practical businessman as well and wasn't about to take a loss, and he didn't think the rifle was worth four hundred. "The rifle isn't enough—I have to lay out money for the new pump."

Tim waffled. "I don't have anything else to trade."

"How about a little cash and the rifle?"

Tim hesitated as if thinking it over—in truth he would sooner part with blood than cash—and while he was pausing he remembered the painting. It was on black velvet, a painting of Elvis riding a white wild horse. He had taken it in on trade thinking it might be worth something.

"I have an original oil painting."

"Of what?"

"It's Elvis, kind of riding a spirit horse, painted on black velvet so it just glows. I took it out of the frame and rolled it up, but you can tack it in a new frame."

And that, wonderfully, strangely, is what did it. Harv, it turned out, was a rabid Elvis fan and when he saw the painting he fairly jumped at it.

By 10:15 that night he had the new fuel pump in the motor home and Tim was on the way out of town.

Harv set the rifle aside and looked at the painting and wondered how it could be that anybody could capture, the King—the dark, brooding eyes, the half-smile—so perfectly on black velvet in colors that seemed to jump off the painting, and no matter which way he turned it the eyes still followed him.

He closed the station at eleven and was nearly out the door with the painting rolled up reverently under his arm when he remembered the rifle.

He took it from the corner, relocked the door, and walked four doors down the side street to where he lived in an old wooden-frame house, where he hung the rifle over the fireplace. His wife didn't think much of it even when told that Tim had said it was a Revolutionary War weapon and she thought less of the painting of Elvis that he wanted to hang above the rifle over the fireplace.

But Harv didn't care. He left the rifle on the nails he'd put in the wall above the mantle and stuck the rolled-up Elvis painting in the top of his bedroom closet until he could get a frame and went to sleep knowing in his heart that he'd done a good business for the day, and here the history of the rifle, in the present, would have ended again, the rifle lying on the nails waiting for the future except for one thing more.

Except for the boy.

The Boy

It is necessary to know this boy.
Born on a crisp fall morning, on October 13, he had some small sickness that made him keep getting ear infections. He seemed to be born pulling at his ear and running a fever, and his parents nearly died of worry when he developed fevers from the ear infection and had to be soaked in a tub of cool water to bring his temperature down to keep the convulsions away during the first two years of his life. Even then he was quiet and rarely

cried unless there was a good reason, like the enormous needles they used for giving him shots to bring the fevers down from the ear infections.

Richard, they named him—Richard Allen Mesington, his first two names after his mother's father, who had never had a son and always wanted one. He was fourteen.

Richard had not always lived in Missouri. He'd been born in Colorado, where his parents lived while his father worked at construction, building houses to sell to the rich people who no longer wanted to live in the cities and moved to the mountains.

For his first six years he lived in a little town named Willow in the mountains west of Denver while his father worked on houses that looked like they belonged in the Swiss Alps.

His childhood was strange for a time because the couple had a small Border collie named Sissy and the boy bonded to the Border collie more than he did to the parents.

Sissy became his baby-sitter and in some ways

his mother, and the boy spent many days in the summer wandering around their house clutching the shoulder fur on the collie while she led him to inspect things that dogs inspect—smelly places, interesting holes in the ground, scents on the wind.

He began to think dog in those days and sometimes, even until he was four, if he was in the yard and smelled a new odor or one that might be from a good taste, he would stop and turn his head to catch the smell on the wind the way a dog does it, trying to see in the direction of the odor, using the smell like a beacon. He, of course, could not smell as well as Sissy but he didn't know that, and when she would stop to smell he would try as well, tottering alongside the dog, moving his nose this way and that to catch the smell.

What made it all stranger was the dog did not truly like the boy. She had been with the couple for two years before the birth of the boy and was jealous of the attention they gave to the child. Often when he had his ear infections and they would go to him in his crib at night, Sissy would stand in their way and try to use her shoulder to keep them from the boy so they would pay attention to her instead.

She would come to love the boy when he was older and she understood that he was simply an extension of the couple, come to love him so much she would have laid down her life for him, but not early, not when he was young. She tolerated the boy along her side, clutching at her hair, and sometimes growled lowly at him when he grabbed too hard and even lifted her lip to him now and then when he was too rough—though she would never, ever bite him—and without thinking led him out of the yard and into the surrounding forest several times.

These little trips terrified the parents, even though Sissy never took him over a hundred yards and he was never gone for over ten minutes. They lived outside of town in the mountains, on the edge of pine forests, and Sissy loved to explore and naturally pulled Richard along until he grew tired and stopped, holding hard to her fur and stopping her.

The parents always found them that way, the boy standing or sitting, tired but quiet, not crying, looking at the woods around them with the dog standing next to him, Sissy not liking it, wanting to be free but caught by the bond of obligation that connects dogs—and especially collies—to humans.

Once she had taken him along a small brook and when the father came upon them, there was the track of a bear in the mud next to the brook and the dog had her hair up and the boy was looking at the green wall of the forest smelling, his nostrils flared and his eyes big, but he didn't talk about what he'd seen or smelled until later that night in his crib.

"Big dog," he said, because he didn't know yet how all words worked. "In woods—*biiig* dog . . ."

When the couple moved to a different house— still in Colorado—there were more children about and he began to have friends other than the dog, and when he stopped hanging on her, the dog had become accustomed to the child being there all the time and stayed with him just the same. Many times the parents would look out the window to see the boy and a small friend playing with their toys in the sand at the side of the driveway and the Border collie sitting there, watching them intently, as if trying to help them play.

One day some heavy equipment moved into the lot next to them, up the side of a hill, and began pushing out dirt to build a house. There was a small bulldozer and a backhoe and a large truck to haul them, and the boy seemed mesmerized, almost smitten with love for the heavy equipment. As soon as he awakened each morning he would run outside and sit on the edge of the property with the collie next to him and watch the men drive the machinery and push the earth.

One morning one of the men came to the house and asked to use the phone to call a concrete truck to keep it from coming because they weren't ready for it. He was a husky man with a tee shirt that barely covered his muscles and was indescribably, to the boy, wonderfully dirty. The man had seen Richard watching them work and he liked children—had two of his own—and he asked the boy's mother if the boy could come up and ride the machinery.

She hesitated at first but saw the excitement in Richard's eyes and decided it would be all right if she went with him and stood to the side to make sure he was all right.

The boy rode both the Cat and the backhoe, and the man let him pull one of the levers on the backhoe to dump the earth from the bucket, and that night when his father came home from work he tried to tell of the excitement of the day but it all jumbled in his mind and mouth and all he could manage was one sentence:

"When I get big I want a bughoe."

And while he still could not formulate the words, he knew then that when he grew if he could just be a driver of heavy equipment and move earth and flatten mounds, there could and would be nothing finer. That Christmas, Santa—he still believed in Santa and would until he was nearly six and saw two Santas, one relieving the other in a shopping mall—brought him heavy metal toys, a truck and a backhoe that picked up dirt to dump in the truck, and for two complete summers he could be found at the edge of the driveway each day, the collie sitting next to him while he made roads, and this would last until he was taken to a dinosaur museum by his grandfather, who loved him so much it was nearly a visible glow. Then the boy wanted to be an archaeologist, which lasted until he was nine and took a flight in a light plane and decided to be a pilot, and that lasted until he saw a show on television—they did not have a television until the boy was ten—about underwater ocean diving and then he wanted to be a scuba diver, and that lasted until he rode a good horse and decided to go to a ranch in Montana and be a cowboy, and that lasted until . . .

He was much like his father, who worked hard all the time but moved from one thing to the next as he learned of them and was devoted and intensely loyal to each of the things as he did them before moving on to the next one.

It was not until the boy was seven that the family moved to Missouri, where the father had a job offer building cabinets and wanted to learn how to be a master carpenter.

In some respects the boy's life in Missouri was the same as it had been in Colorado. They had a nice house in a nice neighborhood, and he had a yard to play in that was safe and the collie came with them. By now he had, of course, quit holding on to Sissy but she had changed drastically and loved him completely—possibly more even than his grandfather—and spent every waking hour watching him, waiting for him to move so she could be with him. She slept next to him on his bed, even went into the bathroom with him, and made him feel at home even though he was in a strange neighborhood where he didn't know anyone.

On the right of their house there was a small frame dwelling painted a spotless white and occupied by an elderly couple. The boy heard that the man had been a fighter pilot in the Second World

War but didn't talk to him until he was of an age to make models, and the man came into his backyard and saw Richard holding a plastic model of a P-51 fighter near the low fence.

"I flew one of those," the man told him, looking over the fence. "You had to be careful in a dive because if the airspeed exceeded the limits the aluminum would start peeling off the upper wing. That's what happened to Johnnie . . ."

And the man told Richard stories of flying in the war, talking to Richard not as if he was a boy but a man, telling him things because he seemed to need to tell these parts of his life to somebody. Richard was fascinated and listened raptly, and from that time on always said hello to the man when he saw him.

On the other side of Richard's house lived Harv Kline. Harv was as nice to Richard as he was to everybody and Richard liked him as much as everybody liked him. He had two children, a boy and a girl, but the boy was three years younger than Richard—the girl still younger—and when Richard was eight the other boy was only five, too young for good playing. The fence between their two yards was only a foot high, a wooden rail, and anytime she couldn't be with Richard, Sissy—who after the years with Richard had decided she was supposed to watch *all* young people—could be found in the Kline's yard playing with and watching Harv's two children.

There were other children on the block and Richard met them and came to know them and one of them became his best friend, a boy named Dennis, and another of them became his first girlfriend when he was nine years old. Her name was Peggy, and it wasn't the same as when he became older, twelve and then thirteen when she became his real girlfriend but even so, even so this first girlfriend business was very serious and he spent hours talking to Dennis about it, telling Dennis how much he loved Peggy though he hadn't told Peggy and indeed would not tell her of his love.

It was all very complicated and Richard thought twice that it would lead to breaking his heart because Peggy didn't seem to notice him and he could not, for the life of him, bring himself to talk to her. He had found that until they moved to Missouri, his life without girls to play with, his life with Sissy the collie had left him almost debilitatingly shy when it came to talking to girls.

It is impossible to guess how long it would have taken him to tell Peggy how he felt but Dennis was a good friend and teasingly told Peggy that Richard loved her and she broke the ice by talking to Richard. She was thin and had a spray of freckles across her nose and straight brown hair that hung down alongside her face, and Richard's tongue stuck to the roof of his mouth whenever she was near.

"Hi," she said. "Dennis said you want to be my boyfriend."

Richard stared at her.

"Is that right?"

He nodded. "I guess so. I mean . . ."

"OK," she said, shrugging, and it was done.

Richard had waited for some change but as far

as he was concerned there was no difference between when he was not Peggy's boyfriend and
when he became her boyfriend, except a little teas-
ing at school and the fact that he tried to make his
shoulders straighter when she was nearby.

And so he grew that way, from nine to ten and
then eleven and twelve and the changes came that
come with growing. Soon he did not play with
small trucks or tractors and instead worked at
models until his room was full of planes and cars
and boats, hanging from the ceiling and on shelves,
and that led to posters, and he fell in love with
baseball and football and basketball all at about the
same time. By the time he was fourteen his mind
was full of stats about players and injuries and
planes and cars and motors and yards gained and
Peggy's eyes and lips and hair and school—where
he turned out to be a slightly above average
student—and performance statistics of cars and a
dream to own a Harley and how to throw a clean
dropping curve and which team would draft which
player the next season and how special effects work

in movies and who was really, really cool and who was not, and his voice had broken and changed and he looked at Peggy differently yet again, wondered at night about her, dreamed about her, and was starting to think that he liked science and would maybe be a doctor or a teacher if he didn't become a major-league pitcher when he was ready for it, and had come to understand and know in his heart that there are no, absolutely no goals that he could not achieve if he put his mind to it and worked hard at it, and he knew that though the time had gone so slow it seemed to stop, he was just getting started, that new things would come as the old ones went and he would grow more and know more, and sometimes it made him smile quietly, just knowing that it was all coming to him and at him, the next day and the next day.

The Joining

It is strange that in all the time of the rifle after John Byam's death and through all the people who looked at it and touched it and handled it, and actually held it to their shoulder as Byam had done, down through the years and years, and even with Tim Harrow, who thought he knew and was an expert at guns and rifles though he did not understand their true place, that nobody, not once in the life of the rifle, did anybody ever think to check to see if it was loaded.

To be sure, it was hard to check. There is not a breech to the rifle, nothing to open to see if there is a cartridge, and in fact there is no cartridge. Powder is poured down the bore and the ball set firmly on top of it. There is no way to simply look and see if the rifle is loaded, and the only way to make certain is to take the ramrod from its bracket beneath the barrel, slide it down the bore until it stops, mark the ramrod where it stops with a pencil, then pull it out and hold it alongside the barrel and see if it goes all the way to the end. If there is a load in the rifle the rod will have stopped well short—up to two inches—of the true bottom of the bore. The method is not widely known to people who have no experience with muzzle-loading weapons and so often it is not known if they are loaded or not.

The rifle was loaded.

When muzzle-loading rifles were in wide use, safety was largely a secondary consideration and there were many accidents. As late as the middle of the nineteenth century, during the Oregon

Trail period, gun accidents along the trail were a leading cause of death and injury. It was, scornfully, thought that an empty rifle was worse than useless if it was needed—because it took so long to load compared to modern weapons—wouldn't even make a good club, and so guns were kept loaded.

Black powder is a strange material. It is easily made in large quantities but is extremely explosive when exposed to sparks or flame or heat. So dangerous is it to store and handle that in the sailing ships of the Revolutionary War, which used black powder for their cannon, the powder magazine was a small room tightly built deep in the center of the ship and no lanterns were allowed in the room though it was always pitch dark. Instead there were sealed windows leading to a second room where the lanterns were kept and the windows allowed the light to come through so the "powder monkeys," small boys who ran from the cannon down to the magazine for powder bags, could come in and work. Even then there were wet blankets hung over the powder room door and the boys had to run beneath the wet blanket—kept wet with constant buckets of seawater—each time they entered or left the magazine. Anything and everything was done to keep a spark or heat from the powder.

Its one saving grace from a standpoint of time is that if black powder is exposed to the air it tends to absorb moisture and water neutralizes and ruins it. Since it is made largely of charcoal, when it absorbs moisture it cakes and becomes inert.

Many things enter into loading a rifle and when John Byam last loaded this rifle he could have done any number of things and they would have insured the powder would cake over the intervening 217 years and turn into a solid lump inside the bore. Had he used a loose patch around the ball, which would allow air to come around the sides, or left the rifle wiped dry of grease so air would work through the tiny hole from the pan—in either case it would have ruined the powder over the long time since he had loaded it.

But John was an expert, and very, very careful. He had used greased mattress ticking for the patch and the grease in the cloth swaged out and made an almost perfect gasket of the cloth. The last British officer he had killed before leaving the front lines had died just as it started to rain, and after loading the rifle John had dabbed just the tiniest amount of grease in the hole from the pan to the charge lest a drop of rain get in the hole. He carried a small sewing needle in his rifle pouch and when he next shot he would first use the needle to clean out the hole so the jet of flame would get through to the charge.

But he never fired again and the grease hardened and solidified in the hole, effectively making an airtight plug.

And so the powder lay for over two hundred years, dry, still in granular form, still ready.

And more bends and twists, turns in time to make it clear when it was done but not before; easy, so easy to see backward but as soon as the vision is moved to the present and then just slightly to the future it fogs and blurs and becomes impossible.

The Christmas season came and with it decorations, and Harv had gotten a box of Christmas things for the station from his distributor as a promotional gift and he put some in the windows at the station but he brought some home. He was always thoughtful and his wife liked candles and in the box there were two elegantly tall candles, red and made of soft wax, set in festive holiday holders, and he brought them home for her as a gift.

"They're perfect for the mantle," she said and put them up over the fireplace in front of the rifle, wishing she had found a way to hide the Elvis painting, which Harv had also hung up over the mantle on the space between the rifle and the ceiling.

"There," she said, "don't they make the house have a Christmas feeling?"

"Along with the tree and presents and two screaming kids—they sure do." And Harv smiled because he meant it and loved this time of the year more than any other.

"I'll light them Christmas Eve," she said, "when we light the fireplace."

CHRISTMAS EVE came two days later and the whole block seemed to light up. Many of the houses had been decorated and some weren't turned on until Christmas Eve, and Richard and his parents walked around the block looking at all the lights.

"It's cold," Richard said, his breath out ahead of him.

"Not as cold as Colorado was," his father said, smiling, and he ruffled Richard's hair and put his arm around his shoulders. "We'll never be that cold again."

They finished their walk and returned to the house where his parents sat in the kitchen to drink a cup of coffee. For a moment Richard stood with them but he thought of the tree that was in the small room next to the kitchen and he went in there to see if any packages had been added to the pile since he last looked at the tree.

LET'S LIGHT the fire." Harv moved to the fireplace, took a box of matches from the mantle, and scratched one, putting it to the paper and pressed wood logs in the fireplace.

"The candles," his wife said. "Light them, too."

He nodded and brought the match up and put it to the candlewick. It sputtered and almost went out, then flared into life. It was placed directly in front of the pan on the rifle, which was hanging over the mantle, and as the flame sputtered a small breeze moved it to the side and closer to the pan. It did not get close enough for the flame to reach the metal but a sliver of heat, almost open flame, came near the touchhole that led to the powder. There was the tiniest bit of old, over two hundred years old, almost mummified grease there blocking the hole and the slight brush of heat was enough to dissolve it and open the way to the powder, but the flame moved away before it could ignite the charge. The flame settled, the flickering stopped, and it rose in a clean brightness toward the ceiling, adding its warmth to the Christmas cheer in the room.

RICHARD MOVED one foot closer to the tree, turned slightly to the right, and raised his right hand to rehook a Christmas tree bulb that seemed to be coming loose.

THE FIRE IN Harv's fireplace was not doing well. The paper and logs lit all right but they were too far forward into the room and the fireplace wasn't drawing well. Smoke drifted out and Harv took a poker from the stand to the side to push the logs back farther into the fireplace, but as he started to do it he stumbled on the corner of the carpet and had to move forward suddenly to keep from falling. The move threw his coordination off and the poker hooked in back of the logs and jerked the top one out onto the floor.

A shower of sparks went up in the air. Most of

them moved up and away from the wall, bounced off the ceiling, and fell to the floor. A half-dozen of them caught a heat eddy and swung inward over the mantle. Of the six sparks, four of them merely bounced off the wall and fell on the mantle to die there.

Two of them got further caught in the heat eddies from the candle flame, and of those two a single one swung in and skipped harmlessly off the barrel of the rifle.

The last spark, almost completely out, cooling fast and no bigger than half the head of a pin, slid off the pan and speared directly into the touchhole of the rifle, where it ran into the sharp edge of a granule of black powder. It nearly died there. For a millionth of a second nothing happened because the powder, so close to the touchhole, had lost some of its explosive properties. Then the spark moved the tiniest part of a distance, no more than a micron, to the left, and found a cleaner, sharper edge of powder. It ignited, if only slightly, but it was enough to double the original spark and that led to other grains of powder and then still more, traveling at a speed so fast it could not be seen, traveling spark to spark at better than twenty-five thousand feet per second, in effect setting the entire charge in the rifle into an instantaneous explosion.

The effect was immediate and stunning. There was an enormously loud crack of sound and the entire living room filled with smoke. Harv looked up, thinking the ceiling had collapsed or that the fireplace had exploded, his wife paused by the door to the kitchen, her eyes wide, both children were frozen on the couch.

"What—," Harv had time to say.

In the meantime the charge, exploding in the confined space of the loaded bore, brought its full force to bear on the only movable object.

The ball had been sitting for over two hundred years, waiting for just this event. The patch had dried, of course, and so didn't provide the lubrication required for a proper shot, but it didn't matter.

With so much pressure—suddenly coming close to eleven thousand pounds per square inch—something had to give and it was the ball.

It left the bore, traveling at a speed of just over twelve hundred feet per second. The front of the ball was pitted by age but that only slowed it slightly and on a longer shot would have made it inaccurate. That did not matter because after traveling only seven feet the ball hit the edge of the window frame in back of the tree, clipping so close to the window itself that it broke the glass in a jagged spider-web pattern as it left the house.

Striking the glass and frame deformed the ball. Had it run true it would have streaked across the space between Harv's house and the next one— where Richard lived—and buried itself in the wall, coming to rest in a two-by-four stud holding the window frame in back of Richard's tree in place.

But being misshaped caused the ball to curve to the side as it flew, hitting almost four inches to the right of the two-by-four, in the glass of the window itself.

The glass moved it a quarter of an inch still more to the right. It clipped through the Christmas tree, cutting four small limbs, grazed the back of Richard's hand as he reached up into the tree to straighten the ornament and struck him in the forehead one inch over his right eye.

The ball had lost some velocity coming through the windows and across the space between the houses but it was still moving at over a thousand feet per second when it hit Richard—faster than bullets leave the barrel of almost all pistols—and it passed through the skull easily, carrying bits of bone with it, destroying the brain almost completely before it passed out the back of his head and finally stopped in the wall next to the door.

All voluntary and involuntary action for Richard ceased instantly. His breathing stopped, his heart stopped after two beats, his brain waves stopped and all his thoughts went blank—he was effectively dead and his world ended by the time his body dropped to the floor next to the tree.

The entire time lapsed from the spark entering

the touchhole of the rifle to Richard dropping dead to the floor was 1.43 seconds, so that Harv still stood, his wife's mouth was still open, his children's eyes were still wide, Richard's parents still sat at the kitchen table, bits of glass were still falling from the broken windows, and Richard was dead, all in less than one and one-half seconds.

And these are the things Richard missed that were in his timeline before it intersected the time-line of the rifle: twenty-one thousand nine hundred sunrises and sunsets, three thousand one hundred twenty-seven movies, nine hundred forty-three baseball games, one hundred fourteen walks with girls on moonlit nights, nine thousand days with warm sun beating down on his back, and swim-ming, hiking, seeing art in museums, watching puppies play, winning a bike race in spite of an injury, graduating from high school at the top of his class, being in the army, graduating from col-lege, getting married in final and true love, grad-uating from medical school as a specialist in research on cardiac-related diseases wherein he would have found a genetic cure for heart disease, having children and watching them grow to have children so he could watch *them* grow, and at last, finally, at seventy-four, becoming ill and dying quietly in his sleep—and all of this, every moment of every day of this, was gone forever with the rifle ball entering his head.

Ended.

The Rifle

It was not done. Not yet.

Richard's parents were torn, destroyed by their grief. His father got counseling and managed to pull himself together enough to continue working as a carpenter but his mother sank further and further into depression, refused all help, and after several thwarted attempts at suicide allowed herself to be committed to the state mental hospital, where she stayed and is now.

Within minutes of the accident Harv found

what the rifle had done, blamed himself, and continued to blame himself until he died four years later in an alcohol-induced vehicular accident when his car hit a bridge abutment. But before that, within weeks of Richard's death, he had driven out of town and stopped at the bridge over Muddy Creek and thrown the rifle in the water and mud to disappear forever—or so he thought.

But a man named Tilson was fishing from the shore beneath the bridge and he saw the rifle fall. He did not recognize it at first as anything but a gun and since he had several guns and was interested, he put a large snag hook on his line and after eleven casts managed to snag the trigger guard and pull the rifle ashore.

He had seen the story in the paper about Richard's death and knew of the accident, of the kind of rifle and that it was antique, and he correctly deduced that this was the rifle. But he thought and believed, as Tim Harrow believed, as millions believe, that guns didn't kill people, people killed people, and he took the rifle home and disassembled it and cleaned it and oiled it until it was almost like new and put it in his walnut-veneer gun case to keep, suspecting it was valuable and a collector's item.

And there it rests now, and would stay that way, except that Tilson read an article in a gun magazine, entitled "Don't Shun That Old Smoke-pole," about shooting with black powder, and he has been thinking seriously about getting some black powder and balls and maybe loading the rifle.

Just to see how it shoots.

And in the meantime the rifle sits in the gun cabinet.

Waiting.

J
PAU

Paulsen, Gary

The rifle

481684

DISCARD

$16.00

DATE			

15(28)

26 01
97
98